THE WATER-BABIES

TOM'S ADVENTURES WITH ELLIE

Tom was swimming round the wonderful island where all the water-babies lived.

Sometimes he couldn't help being naughty. He chased the fish, frightened the crabs and dropped sand and other nasty things into the sea anemones' mouths to make them think their dinner had arrived.

"Take care," the other water-babies warned him. "Mrs Be-done-by-as-you-did is coming."

When Mrs Be-done-by-as-you-did appeared, all the water-babies stood up straight, with their hands behind their backs.

She wore a bonnet and shawl and large spectacles on her hooked nose. She looked at the children and seemed very pleased with them.

She gave them all sorts of nice things like sea cakes, sea apples and sea toffee.

Tom's mouth watered and he hoped his turn would come. At last Mrs Be-done-by-as-you-did called his name and popped something into his mouth.

It tasted *horrible!*

"You are very cruel," cried Tom.

"And you are a very cruel boy, who puts nasty things in the sea anemones' mouths," she said sternly. "As you do to them, so I must do to you."

"And now, be a good boy," she told him. "Then when my sister, Mrs Do-as-you-would-be-done-by comes on Sunday, perhaps she will teach you how to behave."

Tom decided to be a good boy all Saturday. And when Sunday morning came, sure enough, Mrs Do-as-you-would-be-done-by came too.

All the children began dancing and clapping their hands. She had the kindest, prettiest, merriest face Tom ever saw.

"And who are you?" she asked kindly.

"Oh, that is the new water-baby," the others told her.

So she took Tom on her lap and cuddled him while she sang songs and told stories. And she asked Tom, "Will you promise not to torment the sea creatures until I come again?"

So Tom promised. But he found it hard to be good all the time. He was given sweets and began to watch Mrs Be-done-by-as-you-did to see where she kept them. At last he discovered that she stored them in a mother-of-pearl cabinet hidden amongst the rocks.

One night when the other children were asleep, he crept away to the cabinet, and to his surprise the door was unlocked. Inside were all the nice things he longed for.

He tasted one, then another, then gobbled down the whole lot. He didn't know that Mrs Be-done-by-as-you-did was watching him all the time.

The next day, Tom was afraid of what would happen when Mrs Be-done-by-as-you-did found the cupboard empty. But to his surprise, she pulled out just as many sweets as ever, but now Tom hated the taste.

And when Mrs Do-as-you-would-be-done-by came she told him sadly, "I can't cuddle you because you are so prickly."

Tom looked at himself. He had grown prickles all over!

No-one would play with him and he could
do nothing but hide miserably in a corner.
When Mrs Be-done-by-as-you-did came again,
he pushed the sweets away, saying, "No, I can't
bear them now." Then he burst out crying and
told her what he had done.

To his surprise she said, "I will forgive
you, now you've told me the truth."

"And will you take away these nasty
prickles?" he asked.

She shook her head."You put them there
yourself and only you can take them away. I
shall fetch you a schoolmistress who will teach
you how to get rid of your prickles," she
promised.

Tom was afraid his teacher would be very cross and strict, but when she arrived he was astonished. She was the same size as himself, dressed all in silver with long golden hair and the prettiest face.

"There he is," said Mrs Be-done-by-as-you-did, "and you must teach him to be good."

"Do try and help me get rid of my prickles," begged Tom.

So she began to teach him how to behave
properly. Tom learnt very fast and slowly his
prickles vanished.

One day his teacher looked at him and
said, "Why, I know you now. You are the little
chimney sweep who came into my bedroom."

"And I remember you now," cried Tom.
"You are Ellie, the little girl I saw in bed when
I came down the wrong chimney."

Ellie told Tom how the fairies had come for her and brought her away to become a water-baby too.

"And where do you go on Sundays?" asked Tom curiously.

"You must ask the fairies that," said Ellie, "for I am not allowed to tell you. But it is a beautiful place."

"Can I see where Ellie goes on Sundays?" Tom asked Mrs Be-done-by-as-you-did.

"Those who go to that beautiful place must first help somebody they don't like," she said sternly.

"Did Ellie do that?" asked Tom.

"Yes," admitted Ellie. "I didn't like coming here at first and I was afraid of you Tom."

"Because I was covered in prickles?" he asked.

"Yes," she said.

"Perhaps, Tom, you will help someone you don't like," said Mrs Be-done-by-as-you-did, who was looking very worried.

Tom wasn't at all sure about that. But he was afraid Ellie would think him a coward, so he said, "What must I do to help someone I might not like?"

"Go to Mother Carey's Haven and ask her for a special passport," said Mrs Be-done-by-as-you-did. "You must ask all the beasts in the sea and the fowls in the air, and if you have been good to them, they will tell you the way," said Mrs Be-done-by-as-you-did.

So Tom set off on his long journey. He spoke to dolphins, herrings and even the last of the Gairfowl who sat on the All-alone-stone, but none of them could tell him the way to Mother Carey's Haven.

Then along came a flock of petrels, "Come with us and we will show you the way," they cried. "We are Mother Carey's own chickens and she sends us out all over the seas, to show good birds the way home."

Soon the wind began to blow very hard.
They saw a ship, wrecked in the sea. The
petrels flew round it, but Tom heard the sound
of a dog barking and scrambled on board.

On the deck was a terrier, barking and
snapping. Tom wanted to rescue him, but
suddenly a great wave washed over the ship
and swept Tom and the terrier into the sea.

The dog kicked and coughed, then sneezed so hard that he sneezed himself clean out of his skin and turned into a sea-dog. He danced around Tom and swam after him.

Soon they saw the peak of Jan Mayen's Land and there they found a whole flock of molly-mocks.

"This young gentleman is going to see Mother Carey," said the petrels. "But we can take him no further than this as the ice may nip our toes."

Tom told the molly-mocks what he was doing. "You're a plucky one to have got so far," they told him.

The leader took Tom and Sea Dog up on his back and flew off until they could see a gleaming white wall of ice, looming up through the mist and snow and storm.

He set Tom and the sea-dog on the ice below Shiny Wall.

"How am I to get in?" asked Tom.

"Dive underneath if you are brave enough," the molly told him.

"I've not come this far to turn back now," said Tom and he dived into the water with the sea-dog swimming at his heels.

Down and down he went, a thousand fathoms deep, until he could swim underneath Shiny Wall. Then he swam and swam, through deep green waters, until he could see the light overhead.

He came up and through the water and found himself in Peacepool, which is Mother Carey's Haven.

Tom swam up to the nearest whale and asked where he could find Mother Carey.

"There she sits in the middle," said thc whale.

Tom looked, but he could see nothing but one peaked iceberg. Then as he swam nearer, he saw that it was in fact a grand old lady with snow-white hair and eyes as blue as the sea, sitting on a marble throne.

"Please, I've come for a special passport," said Tom.

She showed him a medal on a silver chain with *Mother Carey's Passport* stamped on it.